# ARGUS

## Michelle Knudsen

*illustrated by*

## Andréa Wesson

CANDLEWICK PRESS

Squid life cycle

$S$ally's class was doing a science project. Mrs. Henshaw handed out the eggs.

"Mine looks different," said Sally.

"Now, Sally," said Mrs. Henshaw, "don't be difficult. Some eggs just look different."

The children kept their eggs warm in their brand-new desktop incubators. Soon the hatching began.

"I see a beak!" one boy shouted.

"I see one, too!" the girl next to him called out.

Sally's egg wobbled. A tiny crack appeared. Then another. Something poked out a little bit of shell.

"Is that a beak?" one boy asked.

"I don't think so," said Sally.

The cracks in Sally's egg widened. Slowly, something emerged.

It was green.
And scaly.
And it had big yellow eyes.

"Mine looks different," said Sally.

The other students gathered around to look. "Ewww," they said.

"Now, children," said Mrs. Henshaw, "don't be difficult. Some chicks just, uh, look different—that's all."

Sally named her chick Argus.

Growth Chart for Bruce

Growth Chart for Izzy

Growth Chart for Daisy

Growth Chart for ARGUS

The class weighed and measured all the chicks. They took new measurements every day. Then they made line graphs showing the results.

All of the other children's graphs showed small, neat diagonal lines. Sally's graph . . . didn't.

ARG

Butter

Growth Chart
for
Fluffy

for
Butter

Next the children drew pictures
of their chicks to post on the walls. All
of the other children's pictures were cute
and yellow and very much alike. Sally's
picture . . . wasn't.

"Good work, children," said Mrs. Henshaw. "Now let's investigate what our little chicks like to eat."

"Mine likes seeds!" said one boy.

"Mine likes beetles!" said another.

"Mine is trying to eat the other chicks," said Sally.
Mrs. Henshaw rushed over and rescued them.

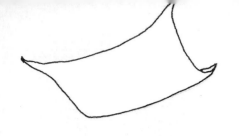

As the days passed, the chicks grew bigger. Argus was the biggest of them all. He stopped trying to eat the other chicks. He started trying to eat the children instead.

"Mrs. Henshaw!" the children complained.

Mrs. Henshaw rushed over and rescued the children.

The students began taking their chicks outside to peck in the grass at recess. Argus wasn't very good at pecking. He chewed a giant hole in the ground with his teeth.

The other chicks all fell into it.
"Mrs. Henshaw!" the children complained.

Mrs. Henshaw rushed over and rescued the chicks. Sally and Argus had to move to a different part of the grass.

Later that afternoon, Sally walked up to Mrs. Henshaw.
"I don't think my chick is working out," she said quietly.

"Now, Sally," said Mrs. Henshaw, "don't be difficult. Just
go ahead and mark your chick's height on the wall with the other
students."

The other children knelt down to mark their chicks' heights.
Sally had to use the stepladder.

The next day at recess, Sally led Argus to his special area. Mrs. Henshaw had marked it off with orange cones for safety. Sally sat and watched the other chicks. They were all the same: cute and small, feathery and fluffy. The children chased them around, picking them up and petting their soft little heads. Sally couldn't even reach Argus's head unless he was lying down.

The bell rang for the end of recess. Sally sighed. She turned around to get Argus.

He wasn't there.

Sally looked around the school yard. She ran to the gate and looked up and down the street. There was no sign of Argus anywhere.

"Oh, no!" cried Sally. She started to run back to class. Then she stopped.

Why was she so upset? With Argus gone, Mrs. Henshaw would probably let Sally share one of the other chicks. She could make graphs that looked just like everyone else's. She wouldn't have to sit by herself at recess. She could stop being different all the time.

Sally lined up to go inside with the other students. She waited to feel relieved. She waited to feel happy.

She kept waiting while she followed the other children down the hallway and back into the classroom.

She waited while she went back to her seat. But she still didn't feel happy or relieved. She felt sad. And worried. What if Argus was scared and lost? He was out there somewhere, all alone.

Slowly, she raised her hand.

"Yes, Sally?" asked Mrs. Henshaw.

"It's Argus," Sally said. "He's gone!"

Then she burst into tears.

The other children gathered around. They held their chicks tightly. "Don't cry, Sally," they said. "We'll help you look for him."

"Yes," said Mrs. Henshaw firmly. "If there's one thing your chick is good at, it's standing out. We'll find him!"

She took down some of Sally's drawings and handed them out to the students.

They searched the neighborhood around the school. They showed the drawings to everyone they met. But no one had seen Argus. Sally got more and more worried. What if they never found him?

Suddenly, they heard a scream. *"Aaaaah!"* someone said. "What is that?"

There was Argus, trying to peck for bugs in someone's front yard.

"Argus!" Sally cried. She ran over and threw her arms around him.

"Our lawn!" said the people whose lawn it was.

"Thank you for finding our lost little chick," Mrs. Henshaw told them.

"But what about these holes?" asked the lawn owners.

Mrs. Henshaw handed them an orange cone. "Don't be difficult," she said. Then she quickly led the children back to school.

My Chick:

eats dirt | sleeps | gets in trouble

How much I love Argus!

Sally

Sally's chart that afternoon was the best one she'd ever made.
Mrs. Henshaw gave it a big gold star. Sally looked at it hanging
up with the other charts. "Mine looks different," she said. And she
smiled.

For Jodi and Sarah for believing

M. K.

For Ben, Gillian, and John

A. W.

First edition 2011

Library of Congress Cataloging-in-Publication Data
is available.

Library of Congress Catalog Card Number pending

ISBN 978-0-7636-3790-3

10 11 12 13 14 15 SCP 10 9 8 7 6 5 4 3 2 1

Printed in Humen, Dongguan, China

This book was typeset in Mrs. Eaves.
The illustrations were done in watercolor and ink.

Candlewick Press
99 Dover Street
Somerville, Massachusetts 02144

visit us at www.candlewick.com